The Fair Housing Five & the Haunted House

Written by the Greater New Orleans Fair Housing Action Center
Illustrated by Sharika Mahdi

Published by the Greater New Orleans Fair Housing Action Center
New Orleans, LA

Hi! My name is Samaria and I'm in the fifth grade.

These are my friends. The five of us like spending time together because we have a lot in common.

Ricardo and James like sports.

Chelsea and Laila like to draw.

James and I like to play music.

Thought Question p.31

The five of us also like spending time together because we are different in a lot of ways.

We have different religions.

We eat different foods.

We have different ways of moving around.

Thought Question p.31

This is our clubhouse. We built it ourselves under an old oak tree. We come here after school to do our homework and play. I like everything about our clubhouse, but it wasn't always that way.

Once upon a time, there was a big, empty house across the street from our clubhouse. We didn't like it at all.

A "For Rent" sign sat out front, but nobody ever moved in. When people visited the house they always left quickly, looking troubled. Every night a single lamp glowed through an upstairs window, and when it was windy out the big iron gate would rattle and shake. We were sure that the house was haunted.

One night I came home and found my mother at the kitchen table with the newspaper spread out in front of her.

"What's going on?" I asked.

She smiled. "It's time for us to move into a new apartment. Why don't you help me look?"

I sat down next to her. There were lots of houses listed on the page. Together we looked at them, one by one. My mom was thinking about grown-up things. "We need a place that's closer to your school and my office. And it needs to be a price we can afford," she said.

I was thinking about kid things. "I want my own bedroom. And I want to live close to my friends," I said.

Thought Question p.31

Finally, we found the perfect place. It had two bedrooms- one for my mom and one for me. It was near the school and not too far from my mom's work. There was a grocery store down the street and a bus stop on the corner. The best part was that it was right across the street from my clubhouse!

I looked closer. *The picture in the paper was of the haunted house!*

The next day we went to see the apartment after school. I was afraid. My mom didn't know that the house was haunted. I gripped her hand as we passed the clanging iron gate. I closed my eyes tight when she rang the doorbell. I heard heavy footsteps, the sound of a lock, and the creak of a door...

"Hi. Are you here to look at the apartment?"

I opened my eyes. It wasn't a ghost, or a monster, or a vampire who stood before us. It was just a regular man. And behind him was a very nice house.

"Hello," my mother said. "This is my daughter, Samaria."

The man's smile vanished instantly. "Oh I'm sorry," he said. "I don't rent to families with children." He shut the door.

My mother shook her head. "Well I guess we'll have to keep looking," she said.

Thought Question p.31

That night I couldn't sleep. I felt confused. Why didn't the **landlord** want to rent to a family with kids? Had I done something wrong? I felt sad. The house was perfect for us, especially now that I knew it wasn't haunted. What if other landlords turned us away? What would we do if we couldn't find a place to live?

The next day I told my friends what had happened. "It just doesn't seem fair," Chelsea said, frowning.

"And why wouldn't someone want to rent to a family with kids in the first place?" added Laila. "Having kids in the neighborhood is good for everyone. Without kids, who would organize kickball games in the park? Who would set up lemonade stands on hot days?"

That gave me an idea. "This calls for a top secret investigation," I said.

Glossary p.30

"We want to know if the landlord is turning away other families.
So let's set up a lemonade stand in front of the clubhouse on
Saturday. We'll use it to spy on the house from across the street!"

And that's exactly what we did.

Saturday morning was quiet. I counted two dog-walkers and three morning joggers, but not one person came in or out of the house across the street.

But all of a sudden, a car pulled up in front, and a woman got out with a kid about our age, and a little baby. We saw her disappear into the house. I wasn't surprised when a few minutes later she came out with a frown on her face.

"Are you going to move into the house?" I asked.

"No, I'm not moving in," the woman said. "The landlord doesn't want to rent to a family with kids. It's too bad, because my son is about your age and you could be friends."

I wanted to tell the woman that I knew how she felt. But I kept my mouth shut because I didn't want to give our top secret investigation away.

Thought Question p.31

One hour, two more dog walkers and a fire engine later, a woman got off the bus on the corner and walked up to the house across the street. She didn't have any children with her. "Surely the landlord will rent to her," I whispered to my friends.

But to my surprise, the woman was back out on the street in no time. "Are you going to move into the house?" I asked.

"No, I'm not moving in," the woman huffed. "The landlord thought I would prefer to live in a neighborhood with more people *like me.*"

"What does that mean?" I asked, confused.

The woman frowned. "I don't think he rents to black people."

I looked around at my friends. All of us were different **races**. Why did it matter?

Thought Question p.31   Glossary   p.30

Two hours, three more joggers and an ice cream truck later, a man walked up with his dog. This man was white like the landlord and didn't have any kids with him. "Surely the landlord will rent to him," I whispered to my friends.

But to my surprise, a couple minutes later the man was back out on the sidewalk. "Are you going to move into the house?" I asked.

"No, I'm not moving in." The man shrugged, and patted his dog. "I'm blind, and my guide dog helps me get around. But the landlord says I'm not allowed to keep a dog in the house, so I can't live here."

I thought about people I knew who needed certain things to get around because of their **disabilities**. Why should they be treated any differently?

Thought Question p.31   Glossary p.30

As the sun began to set, we were sure that something was wrong.

Why would the landlord turn away so many nice people, just because of their race, disability, or the fact that they had kids?

"Maybe he wants to keep certain kinds of people from moving to the neighborhood," James said.

That made me angry. "That's not fair! It's our neighborhood too," I cried. After all, our clubhouse was across the street.

On the way home I thought about how my mom and I still didn't have a place to live.

Thought Question p.31

In school the next day, Ms. Butler was teaching a history lesson.

"Once, not too long ago, black people in our country couldn't live in certain neighborhoods just because of their race," she told us. "Now what are some reasons people choose to live where they do?"

I knew the answer to this question. My mom and I had just talked about it! "Well, my mom and I need to live close to school and her work," I said. "And we need a place with two bedrooms that we can afford."

"Yes," said Ms. Butler, "Those are important things to think about when choosing a home. Now what if someone took away your opportunity to choose? How would it feel if someone decided that a house wasn't right for your family just because of your race or religion, because your family has kids, or because you have a disability?"

I knew the answer to that question too. "I would feel sad and upset," I said. "And things would be a lot harder for my family."

Ms. Butler explained that when someone takes away opportunities from a group of people just because of who they are, that's called **discrimination**. Discrimination makes life harder for a lot of families. Many brave people have fought to stop it.

She told us how Dr. Martin Luther King Jr. led marches into neighborhoods where black people were not welcome. "The marchers were folks just like us who stood strong in the belief that discrimination is wrong," she said.

Because of their courage, there are now rules against discrimination in housing.

I snuck a glance at my friends. Suddenly everything was making sense. I raised my hand.

Glossary p.30   Thought Question p.31

"My mom and I tried to rent a house, and the landlord told us he doesn't rent to families with kids," I said. Then I told her about our top secret investigation.

When I was done, Ms. Butler smiled. "Even though discrimination is against the rules, it still happens. When you get home from school, tell your mom to call the **Fair Housing Center**. They help people who are treated unfairly when they are looking for a home."

Glossary  p.30

I did just that. My mom called the Fair Housing Center, and they listened to our story.

A week later, we got a call back. Using our investigation, the Fair Housing Center proved the landlord was discriminating! They were going to work with us and the landlord to make sure that my mom and I could move into the apartment.

I couldn't wait to tell my friends and Ms. Butler the next day.

"Thanks to us, the Fair Housing Center will make sure the landlord treats people fairly from now on," I told them after class.

"Congratulations," said Ms. Butler. "You all really made a difference. You should call yourselves the Fair Housing Five!"

Thought Question p.31

Back at the clubhouse we celebrated and made plans. "We should tell our families about fair housing," said Ricardo.

"And our friends at school!" added James.

Just then there was a knock on the door. Who could it be? Didn't they see the sign to "Keep Out?" We couldn't let just *anyone* in.

But then I remembered what it felt like to be turned away from a house I wanted to live in. If houses should be open to everyone... so should our clubhouse.

I opened the door wide. "Come on in," I smiled. "My name is Samaria. We have some very important work to do. Want to help?"

Thought Question p.31

Glossary

Disability: A disability is a unique way in which a person's mind or body works. A person with a disability might complete everyday activities like moving, reading, or speaking, differently. *James can't walk because of his disability, so he uses a wheelchair. The man Samaria meets at the house is blind, so he uses a guide dog.*

Discrimination: Discrimination is taking away opportunities from a group of people, or treating them badly, just because of who they are. *Samaria and her mother experience discrimination because their family has kids.*

Fair Housing: Fair housing is the idea that all people should be able to rent or buy a home that meets their needs, even if they are different. *Samaria and the people she meets during her investigation may be different than the landlord, but they should still be able to rent his apartment.*

Fair Housing Center: A fair housing center is a group of people who work together to help those who are unfairly turned away from housing. *Samaria and her mom call the Fair Housing Center when they are treated unfairly.*

Landlord: A landlord is a person who owns a home and lets somebody else live there for a fee. The fee is called rent. *The Fair Housing Center will make sure that the landlord treats people fairly from now on.*

Nationality: Nationality describes the country a person or her family or is from. *Ricardo's nationality is Mexican because his family is from Mexico. Chelsea's nationality is Vietnamese because her family is from Vietnam.*

Race: Race is a way to group people sometimes based on how they look or where they're from. Race is a make believe idea but it has real effects, like discrimination. *Samaria is black and James is white.*

Page 4: Think about one of your friends. In what ways are you alike? What do you like to do together?

Page 5: Think about one of your friends. In what ways are you different? What have you learned from him or her? What have you taught him or her?

Page 8: What does your family need in a house or apartment and why? What would your ideal house or apartment look like?

Page 11: How would you feel if you were in Samaria's situation?

Page 15: How do you feel about the way the landlord treated the family? Is he being fair? Why or why not?

Page 17: How do you feel about the way the landlord treated the woman? Is he being fair? Why or why not?

Page 19: How do you feel about the way the landlord treated the man? Is he being fair? Why or why not?

Page 21: What would you do if you were in Samaria's situation?

Page 24: Have you ever experienced discrimination? How did it feel? If you have not experienced discrimination, what do you imagine it would feel like?

Page 26: What could you do to make people feel welcome in your neighborhood?

Page 29: Look at the picture. What is the important work Samaria and her friends must do? Why?

After reading: Why is fair housing important? What can you do to stop discrimination in your community?

For our future leaders in the struggle for justice and equity:
Samaria and Teren Smothers
& Ms. Monique and Ms. Rowan's 2009/2010 class at Audubon Charter

Special thanks to Monique Butler, Rowan Shafer, Crissy Moore, Vera Warren-Williams, Jennifer Turner, Aesha Rasheed, Lauren Bierbaum, Kelly Harris, Catherine Robbin, Alice Spencer, JoAnn Clarey, Shannon del Corral, Freddi Evans, Kathleen Whalen, Charles Tubre, Cindy Singletary, Audubon Charter School, Eisenhower Elementary School, Alice Harte Charter School, Urban League College Track, and countless other individuals who have supported this project. This project was financially assisted by the Louisiana Bar Foundation.

ISBN: 0-615-41912-7

Published in 2010 by the Greater New Orleans Fair Housing Action Center
404 S. Jefferson Davis Pkwy
New Orleans, LA 70119
(504) 596-2100
www.gnofairhousing.org

The text is set in Bookman Old Style with titles in Giddyup
The illustrations are rendered in acrylic paint on illustration board and canvas
The design is by Hannah Adams

About the Author:

The Greater New Orleans Fair Housing Action Center is a private, non-profit civil rights organization established in the summer of 1995 to eradicate housing discrimination throughout the greater New Orleans area. Through education, investigation, and enforcement activities, GNOFHAC promotes fair competition throughout the housing marketplace.

GNOFHAC is dedicated to fighting housing discrimination not only because it is illegal, but also because it is a divisive force that perpetuates poverty, segregation, ignorance, fear, and hatred.

Learn more about fair housing at www.gnofairhousing.org

About the Illustrator:

Sharika Mahdi-Neville grew up in New Orleans' Ninth Ward. Sharika has embraced art since childhood, spending hours listening to music and drawing figurative images. Moving beyond drawing, she discovered painting in high school where art classes became the platform on which she would stand to unite with the world-renowned art guild, Young Aspirations /Young Artists Inc, (YA/YA) which provided her with training and exposure to art. Sharika earned an undergraduate and a graduate degree in Mass Communication from Louisiana State University.

Sharika's work is described as "happy" and has been praised by Charles Bibbs and Maya Angelou. Her love for kids and education inspired her work on *The Fair Housing Five*.

See more of Sharika's art at www.sharikamahdi.com

About the Book:

Developed by the Greater New Orleans Fair Housing Action Center in collaboration with New Orleans educators, parents and students through a series of workshops and focus groups, *The Fair Housing Five* is the story of kids who take action in their neighborhood in response to a landlord who is treating people unfairly. It is a book designed to initiate dialogue between parents, caregivers, teachers and children about discrimination, inequality, and the important role that we all have in ending both.

Learn more about the book and available workshops at www.fairhousingfive.org

About Fair Housing:

The Fair Housing Act protects people from discrimination in housing based on race, color, religion, sex, national origin, familial status (having children), and disability. Discrimination is illegal in all housing transactions, including rental, sales, lending and insurance.

If you have been discriminated against, contact the fair housing center near you.

Published by FastPencil

http://www.fastpencil.com

DATE DUE

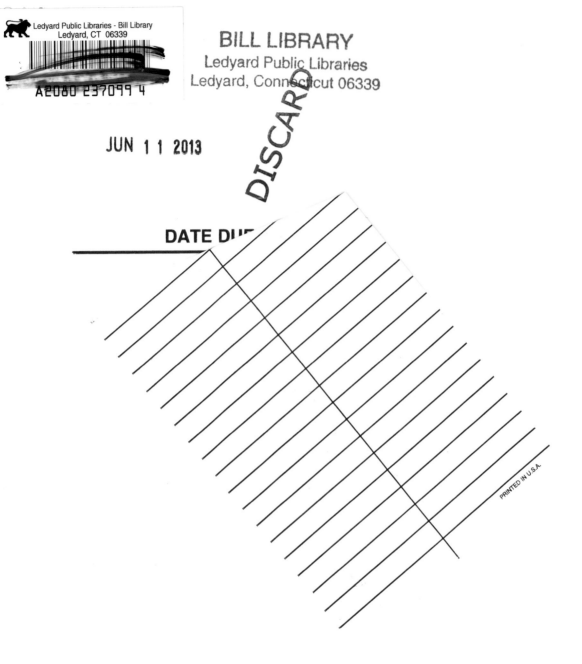

PRINTED IN U.S.A.